CW00864614

Charlotte Godkin is a humorous lady who certainly lives in the world of fantasy. Her knowledge and imagination are expressed in this book. Charlotte lives in Northumberland close to the moors, where she is often seen walking her Chihuahua, gathering thoughts and wild flowers for her next book.

Book 1: Life and Times of Miss Daisy Weed

Book 2: Miss Daisy Weed Down to Earth

Book 3: Miss Daisy Weed's Other Half

Book 4: Miss Daisy Weed's Flower Power

Book 5: Miss Daisy Weed's Heat Wave Experience

Book 6: Miss Daisy Weed's Little Piece of Heaven

CHARLOTTE GODKIN

MISS DAISY WEED'S OTHER HALF

AUSTIN MACAULEY PUBLISHERS™
LONDON • CAMBRIDGE • NEW YORK • SHARJAH

Ordering Information
Quantity sales: Special discounts are available on quantity purchases by corporations, associations, and others. For details, contact the publisher at the address below.

Publisher's Cataloging-in-Publication data
Godkin, Charlotte
Miss Daisy Weed's Other Half

ISBN 9781641827522 (Paperback)
ISBN 9781641827539 (Hardback)
ISBN 9781645364719 (ePub e-book)

Library of Congress Control Number: 2021900561

www.austinmacauley.com/us

First Published (2021)
Austin Macauley Publishers LLC
40 Wall Street, 33rd Floor, Suite 3302
New York, NY 10005
USA

mail-usa@austinmacauley.com
+1 (646) 5125767

To

Dr. and Mrs. R Anderson and son Richard,
Dr. and Mrs. A. Armstrong,
and to Simon Hadden for all his encouragement.

Also dedicated to Elizabeth Christine, my valued and treasured friend and to all my friends at St. Mary the Virgin, my village church.

Thanks to Austin Macauley Publishers for all their support and guidance.

Table of Contents

Introduction
Miss Daisy Weed's Other Half

Miss Daisy Weed had certainly blossomed in Mr. Hill's garden, she felt incredibly fortunate as she had all she ever wanted. She felt relaxed and content for the first time. She knew, also for the first time, what she wanted out of her life. In the past she had always been torn apart by a definite urge she had no control over, which appeared to lead her to destruction. Although she could see her misguided ways, it was only since the earth moved in Mr. Hill's garden that she was able to have this peace within her. Although so much stronger and wiser, Miss Daisy Weed could not remember very much, she had faint recollection of the fairies' treatment ring in Fairy Glen.Thankfully she had no memory of Stanley and the spade which had completely halved her. The spider Horace, however, was a different thing, she remembered him all too well and looked with interest for his return. Rude spider, she thought. She was never quite sure if she had seen him under a leaf beside Clover, who was still her very best friend, but it was all hazy that bit, as she had fallen asleep. It had been very hard to keep awake whilst recovering, even with the help of the fairies at the bottom of the garden and all their fairy dust sprinkled constantly on her. Miss Daisy Weed was the smaller half, so she had to grow and fade and grow again, before she became a complete daisy once again. The wild flower garden, Mr. Hill had decided on, was where Clover and Miss Daisy Weed resided, growing everyday stronger, growing side by side.

A tap was fitted to a newly built stone wall behind them and each day at approximately the same time, after the sun went down, Mr. Hill or his gardener arrived to turn the tap on and a delicious sprinkling of stream water sprayed over them all. All was the right word to use, as Miss Daisy Weed had blossomed and spread almost as large as Clover and his siblings. Miss Daisy Weed had no sooner become whole again that she noticed several buds and leaves appearing around her and still spreading. Miss Daisy Weed had never felt happier and although she missed her other half, in truth, she was happier without her. The garden seemed to improve everyday as Mr. Hill had new ideas and was constantly busy changing or adding to his precious garden. Even when Mr. Hill left his garden down the winding path, he could still be seen by the ever-growing plants, as he sat in his Victorian conservatory reading his papers, or snoozing and then he would, more often than not, return to the garden. He had just recently purchased a white wrought iron garden seat, this was place against the stone wall close to the tap. It was the best position for the seat, as it was sunny and the stone gave off warmth and protection from the wind. The latest addition to the garden were two apple trees, they were in extremely large terracotta pots placed either side of the lily pond. However, he had moved them around a bit, as they had been originally purchased for either side of his conservatory. Mr. Hill had changed quite a lot as he grew older, he just wanted peace and tranquility and certainly not the bowls that he used to love, or even want the temptation of his neighbor Judge Arthur's whiskey decanter. The latter he gave into more often than he cared to remember, but Mr. Hill's garden took precedence over all others.

Chapter One
The Good Blossom, the Bad Flourish

Johnny Brown spotted Miss Daisy Weed twisted in his bicycle wheel, after a good hour of cycling. He arrived at the very top of the hill and was looking forward to a relaxed, free wheel downhill. Johnny Brown's mind was on other things, mainly the events including the young daughter of Mr. Hill, Sally Hill, he cringed as he thought of parading boldly holding her hand and all the humiliation that succeeded such an innocent date. How was he to know she was twelve years old? Well, he was not quite nineteen and anyone could make that mistake. He just could not really get it out of his mind, nor could he justify it, he knew there was something not quite right.The wind had changed directions in fact, the sky had a look of a storm and then it happened, the wind blew full force at his face and full force at Miss Daisy Weed. Within seconds the weed had twisted around the wheel in several places and the roots, still attached, had twisted around Johnny's trainer and right pedal, as he free wheeled downhill. As he approached a bridge, notorious for accidents, he totally panicked as he thought a snake was entwined around his foot and heading up his trouser leg. The language that came out of Johnny Brown's mouth was second to none, followed by a cry for help and also his treasured bike, as he appeared to dive over the side of the stone bridge. Normally when Johnny Brown put a stepwrong, everyone knew, but not this time. He stood in water past his neck but no oneappeared to have seen or heard.

Poor Johnny could only dream of the swimming lessons he had not bothered with and all the warnings he had received, almost identical to this moment in time. He clung desperately to a warning sign marked 'Danger, no swimming,' which was under the arch of the bridge, not having any idea what to do. As normal in Johnny Brown's life, fate took over, the clouds opened and a storm to beat all storms began and seemed as if it would never end. Johnny shivered and prayed as he felt the end of his existence on the planet was in sight. He cursed Sally Hill as he justified his own innocence and blamed her for far more than the trickery of her age, including his high diving into this deep and now becoming flooded river. His rage was rewarded as the 'Danger' warning post he clung to snapped and off he went once again, through the arch and down the fast-flowing river. Johnny closed his eyes, but he really did not need to, as very quickly he was on a sand bank; wet, scratched, but safe.

As Johnny pulled himself together mentally and climbed up the bank of the river and over the fence on to the road, to his surprise no one appeared to be any the wiser of his dramatic escape from drowning. Apart from a few cows that seemed to glance over from a hedge on the opposite side of the road and two cyclists, there appeared to be no one around to talk to about his dreadful ordeal. So Johnny set out to walk to the nearest village and ask for help to return home.

Very soon the storm had ceased and the flooded river was starting to return to normal. Farmer Adam parked his tractor and stood looking over the bridge at the fast-flowing river.

His farm land joined the river on either side, so he was making sure no cattle had been washed down the river, as it had certainly been quite a storm. He looked and squinted, not sure what he was looking at, as the sun that had suddenly come out was quite blinding. Farmer Adam decided to take a closer look and to his delight, there was Johnny Brown's bike; rather scratched and with weeds twisted in the front wheel, but a rather good blue bike. He was delighted and pulled it out of the mud verge and river and placed it on his tractor. Later Miss Daisy Weed was placed in a rather bad smelling cow shed, she was still attached to the wheel.
Miss Daisy Weed slept sound and awoke early morning when a very friendly cow came to look at her. She was not afraid as diving into the river, roots and all, took some beating. So she stared back at this curious cow, who did not appear to know whether to eat her or make a friend of her. Miss Daisy Weed relaxed, her head resting on the inside wheel of the bike. It truly was quite comfortable, no different from being in a flower pot as her roots were still saturated after her swim in the flooded stream, as she decided that was what she had experienced. The cow smiled at her and seemed to be speaking a cow language she had never heard before. The cow shook her head, as she heard Farmer Adam, call her name for milking, "Daisy! Come on girl," and Daisy the cow, obediently turned and skipped off towards the milking shed, which was the next shed to Miss Daisy Weed. A small bell around the cow's neck rang softly in the air. Miss Daisy Weed was astonished, so this is how daisies become cows.

She looked down at herself to see if there was any similarity, her roots were certainly brown like the cows and they did have similar smiles, but that was where the likeness ended.

Miss Daisy Weed slept a little and waited for the return of the cow with interest. Daisy the cow returned a little later, feeling lighter and hungry. She looked at Miss Daisy Weed and although her tummy rumbled and although she did not relish her indoor food supplied by the local farm shop, she still did not think of eating Miss Daisy Weed.

Daisy the cow never could differentiate between what her body passed out to what she put in, as it all smelt the same to her. Although, texture was very different! She decided to go out into the fields and eat some of the delicious smelling grass. She sniffed Miss Daisy Weed and as the she turned to go, the little bell around her neck caught the roots of Miss Daisy Weed and off they both skipped, down the field, towards the soft earth at the top of the river bank. The cow's hooves sunk into the soft sandy earth and as she stepped firmly onto more solid ground, she shook her little bell to ward off any flies from landing on her, as there appeared to be quite a few out this morning after the storm the day before. Miss Daisy Weed dropped, rather than was flung, from the cow's bell and landed safe and extremely comfortable, yet again in the moist soft earth. The cow hoofed the ground around Miss Daisy Weed and then went off to eat some breakfast. Miss Daisy Weed, feeling so safe and very important in her new river side home, where she had views from every direction, drank a little water and slept in the morning sun. The cow returned later in the morning then disappeared again later in the day, for yet again another milking.

It was perfect! The ground never seemed to be too dry or too wet, it was never to sunny, windy or wet, it was just perfect as far as Miss Daisy Weed was concerned. Really it was all she ever wanted; an adventure, a little companion and a new home, where the grass was greener, with scenic views.Miss Daisy Weed flourished and in no time at all, had not grown into a cow, but certainly had grown and spread, as buds and leaves appeared covering the ground around her. So that was Miss Daisy Weed's life and although she had wanted more of a selfish life for herself; doing what she wanted and not missing out on anything exciting, her life became more the opposite; providing wisdom and caring for her rather large bunch of unruly, demanding siblings.Miss Daisy Weed did not grow into a cow, but the sweet Daisy cow and Miss Daisy Weed spent every moment they could together. The bond they had started that sunny morning, after the dramatic journey on Johnny Brown's bike, from Mr. Hill's garden to this remote piece of land, beside the river that had changed her life forever, bonded the two Daisy named friends in eternal love.Meanwhile Miss Daisy Weed's other half was still very content and blossoming in Mr. Hill's garden.

Chapter Two
Hero Worship

The lily pond was incredible! Mr. Hill had planted, with the help of his gardener, the correct plants to compliment his rather unusual pond. It was oblong with each four corners taking on slightly different shape. He had a small white wooden bridge going over the middle. There were water rushes and special water weeds, some to help clean the pond and some to give nutrients to the goldfish. Lily had expanded so there were several new lilies, not quite as large as the original who was loved by all in the garden and made so welcome when after the conservatory had been built, had been moved into this man-made pond. Lily's old pond, where she had lived happily for as long as she could remember, had been polluted so she was delighted with her new and extremely safe pond. The goldfish had also increased in number by at least a dozen or more, some new little fish and some fully grown, constantly swam around Lily and often splashed her. Lily loved them as Lily loved company and loved to talk. Goldie was still swimming around with his mother close on his tale. He was the hero and always would be to his proud mother, who told all the new goldfish the story, of how her son Goldie had led them all to safety after the contamination. Goldie was a bit older now and did not enjoy the attention as much as he used to, in fact he was starting to resent his mother Silver following him around. He felt like a big fish in a small pond.

It seemed to Goldie this was his life forever, until a little while ago, on a very stormy evening, Mr. Hill came into the garden with a small plastic bag, he then placed the bag over the pond and emptied the contents and out she splashed, the most beautiful goldfish Goldie had ever seen. He looked at her fish eyes and there was immediate connection between them. Copper, the new goldfish, who was more copper colored than gold was exquisite; perfect fins and a tail so long and elegant. She had cried in the weeds that night for her siblings, they were still in the pet shop as they were not as attractive as she was. When Goldie heard her crying, he swam to her aid and comforted her until the morning light. Silver, who knew love when she saw it, swam out of sight of the two love fish. Goldie was so happy and with Lily and Silver's advice and help, set up home in the weeds together. Copper was friendly, shy, helpful, and so appreciated everything including her new mom, Silver. It was in such a short time that even more, not purchased, goldfish arrived. Goldie and Copper were the proud parents of Bronze, White Gold and Steel. They were in fish heaven, in the lily pond Silver fish sat, when they wanted to swim to the far side of the pond and play in the weeds. Goldie however, feeling a little left out as all the attention went to his family, decided his imaginary pains were coming back. So, although he was a hero, it appeared he had not changed his spots that much.

Chapter Three
Arthritic Spider

Horace the spider sat in the clover leaves very close to Miss Daisy Weed and all her siblings. He curled up, relaxed, as he viewed the rather pretty daisy. It did not make sense to Horace, where was the daisy's other half? It was very confusing to poor Horace. Miss Daisy Weed showed no malice to Horace for laughing at her when she was so badly injured, she realized it was just his spider ways, besides he had rather a nice laugh and she was also starting to enjoy his company, that appeared to be getting less and less. Horace had his own big problems at home, as his mother's independence became less and the responsibilities of her care rested solely on him.Spider mom, who had spent many a day or night down a slimy drain, always had problems with her legs. At first she put it down to the many times she had given birth. She often reminded Horace, on a day when she wanted him to mend her web, or bring some shopping for her, how hard it had been running after all these crawling young spiders. "The crawling everywhere never seemed to stop!" she would say. So poor mommy spider had arthritis in her four back legs. Horace had lots to do, catching extra insects and a few moths, which he carried carefully to his mommy spider's home and tried to do this shopping at least twice a week. It was tiring but rewarding as he loved his Spider Mom and loved her constant storytelling.

Horace curled up beside his mom listening to how she arrived, where she now lived. She was never sure how long she had lived in this area, but knew it was long enough to have several litters of spiders. She often saw all her now almost fully grown spiders, as spiders never strayed far away from their webs and from a young age were taught to make their web. It was an old outhouse at the back of Lucy's house, it had been an old washroom, where maids would have done household chores. There were only a few Georgian houses in the lane, which had been a very wealthy lane, mainly owned by millers and shipping owners. The backs of the houses were closer to each other than the fronts, as when first built the houses were for one very rich and wealthy family,
with a title. It was perfect for spiders as they could roam around safely at the backs of these houses without danger. It was only Horace that had decided he was worthy of the front entrance of these lovely homes. Spider Mom warned Horace often how it only took a human foot in the wrong place and a spider's existence was over. However, Horace did more taxi runs than crawling, so he felt quite safe. Spider Mom continued her storytelling how she came to live here. She used to live in a potting shed, which was a very common place for spiders to live, she was just to the left of where the door opened in and across the corner. She was fairly content. A man called Edward frequented the shed, always busy potting and mommy spider enjoyed watching him especially when she had her baby spiders and was confined to her web.

It was entertaining and good company, most spiders like humans, it's just that most humans don't like spiders. It was a cold evening in late September, Edward had lived alone since his wife had died after the birth of his daughter. Sarah, his daughter was his life but after her University degree had settled with her boyfriend an hour from where she used to live with her father.This meant that Edward had to catch the eight o'clock train on a Friday night to stay with Sarah for the weekend. Edward had been totally carried away potting some broccoli, his favorite, he had omitted to check the time and when he did it was seven forty leaving him very little time. So rushing from his shed, he suddenly remembered his bunch of keys. It was starting to get dark and as he put his hand around the door of the shed and felt for his keys, he inadvertently swept a huge web complete with Spider Mom and placed it in his green jacket pocket, he then pulled the zip along for safety. After a pleasurable train journey, Spider Mom was hauled out of the pocket on the hanky she had snuggled up in. Edward who was not used to the clean air of this countryside, was about to sneeze, very loudly. Spider Mom dropped out and landed on the top of Edward's suitcase that he wheeled at quite a speed, in haste to see his daughter and off she went the case bumping into every loose, lose stone and curb. Spider Mom feeling quite sick from all this traveling decided to take her chance and exit the top of the case, that she was already slipping down from.At the end of these large Georgian houses there was a high stone wall, this was Lucy's mother's house. As the case got closer to the stone wall, Spider Mom spotted a huge spider web, it was one of the finest she had ever seen, it shone in the full moon, various colors displaying as glimpses of the insects caught the light.

This was where Spider Mom dropped from the case and crawled at speed towards the web. On closer inspection it was a masterpiece of art, it was perfect and the large handsome spider sat behind the web smiling at his new visitor, was no easy catch. He took Spider Mom's breath away, he was everything she had ever dreamed of. She could not believe her luck when he asked her to move into his home behind his web. She had many litters of spiders with this handsome unnamed spider. Then one morning when she woke, he had gone. She looked around for him but could not leave her young spiders too long. So she was never sure what had happened, all she knew was she was sad, so as soon as her small spiders grew, off they all went following their mommy spider, as they looked for a new home. It took no time at all to find the out building at the back of the house and in they all went. Webs were made immediately by Spider Mom who proudly showed her offsprings, her creative skills. Horace who was more like his father than any of the others, was her favorite. So poor willing Horace was called on to bring and fetch food by his mother.

Miss Daisy Weed tried to get Horace to talk to her on the few occasions he came to visit her, but he seemed too tired to talk, let alone laugh. Sometimes he curled up with his legs wrapped around her stem and fell promptly asleep. Miss Daisy Weed loved that, it was a lovely reassuring feeling that this poor spider trusted her enough to be able not only to relax around her but to sleep. Clover looked at Miss Daisy Weed with complete admiration. She had been through so much, yet all she could think about was the welfare and happiness of others on the planet, including this extremely tired spider.

Chapter Four
Two Halves Make a Whole

Miss Daisy Weed slept soundly. Horace, his legs wrapped around her stem, slept, and Clover leaning close to her, his roots touching her roots, also slept. It really was a beautiful sight,
so peaceful, in the midday sun.Miss Daisy Weed's other half slept soundly also, her stem and petals a little crushed, as Daisy the cow slept, her front legs one at either side of Miss Daisy Weed and although one leg overlapped her a little, it did not hurt as the soft earth beneath made a cushion, it was a peaceful and perfect sight.The two daisies were one and although they never really knew just how much they behaved as one, their many dreams manifested their oneness and today was no different. Horace dreamt simply of Lucy laughing happily, his mother crawling, her legs healed, his father returning and Miss Daisy Weed meeting her other half. Clover blissfully slept, he was at peace with the world, all his prayers had been answered and he thanked God, especially for the return of his true love Miss Daisy Weed. Daisy the cow dreamt of sunshine and skipping down field after field and Miss Daisy Weed smiling, as she heard her bell jingle. The two daisies met and hugged each other, tears dripping on their mirror image faces. Their petals touched and they moved together towards a large beautiful butterfly, it was Fluffy from the Amazon Rainforest, she beckoned them to rest on her wings. So one sat on each wing they set off on an adventure of love, love to each other and love to all living creatures and plants.

Where the two Miss Daisy Weeds landed, the forest seemed to be alive, the trees moved as if swaying a greeting to them, little furry animals sounded cries of happiness at their arrival. The two daisies set off one going one way and one the other, no words were spoken between them as words were never needed between them. They knew each other as they knew themselves!They recognized trees they had met from the past and birds some so large their wingspan blocked the sunlight as they swiftly flew under the trees and landed on their familiar branches, as they looked down on the two daisies that had come to help. Miss Daisy Weed's love floated in the air, up and around the trees and incredible plants, never seen anywhere else but in this dense rainforest, when touched by their love, seemed to grow greener and stronger in front of their eyes. There were toadstools which normally would have helped the roots of the trees, dried up and broken, after the daisies' healing was quickly refreshed, their dehydration completely gone and their thirst quenched, ready to do their job healing the trees. Then very soon the leaves on the trees seemed to return in abundance with berries and minerals.

The birds soon became aware of the available food and sung and chirped in gratitude. The furry animals that lived high up in the trees suddenly appeared, they had feared for their life, from hunger and hunters as they were weak and hungry, vulnerable to creditors. The insects that appeared worm-like and blended into the color of the bark of the trees, had dried and lay dead, almost part of the bark. It was such a sad sight and what was worse brought about from greed.

The significance of this was not yet understood by the daisies they just somehow knew! As they travelled down the tree there appeared to be some insects alive, yet struggling in the stifling heat. The daisies quickly refreshed the bark and insects. Then on the ground they spotted a magnificent furry Mura's tamarin monkey, he was crying, his mother had been stolen by poachers, who would sell her for amusement as a family pet. Miss Daisy Weed went close and comforted him, then after feeding him a banana helped him onto a lower branch of an amazing red bark tree. The baby monkey understood and wiping his eyes made off up into the higher branches. Miss Daisy Weed who was working her love and healing the opposite side of the forest had come across a small jaguar, his mother had been killed, shot for her skin in a cruel attack by humans to sell her coat to make bags and accessories.

The poor cub was dazed, Miss Daisy Weed was at a loss what to do. Suddenly she spotted three jaguar cubs coming towards her, they also told her what the poachers had done to their mothers. Miss Daisy wept and started to understand the word greed. She introduced the three cubs to the other cub and after she had prayed to God, the creator of all, she suddenly knew she had to help these babies. She told them to stay together and listen carefully to unusual noises and hide. Yet, she knew only prayers and love in the world would protect these wonderful trusting animals. They seemed a little happier as they went on their way and Miss Daisy Weed promised to see them again.

A snake lay at her feet, he a was pale green anaconda toad-headed snake and he appeared blind. Miss Daisy spoke softly and gave her love, she had lost her husband in the forest! Miss Daisy Weed quickly helped this romantic sad snake as she had seen a snake just like her, where she had landed with Fluffy. She told the tearful snake and off she went at incredible speed to find her husband. That made Miss Daisy Weed happy for a while, only a while, as soon she was sad again when she discovered another baby monkey. He had fallen from high up a tree as the dried up branch had snapped. His mother who was teaching him to swing from branch to branch and had not understood that the branches were dried and the baby had fallen with the branch down the tree. Fortunately, the branch he clung to kept stopping as hit other branches beneath, so his fall had been broken. Miss Daisy Weed dusted him down and petted him with her petals. The monkey laughed and giggled and then suddenly his mother swung close holding on to a huge branch and grasped her baby in her other arm and up and away they went into the tree once again. Miss Daisy Weed smiled and moved on. A baby songbird that although was only a few weeks old, was trying so hard to fly higher than his wings would take him. He explained how his mother and siblings and lots of other birds of the same breed were leaving the dried up, yet still beautiful rainforest. The birds were migrating, going to United States for the summer, so they could grow without fear of hunger and such danger as the forest seemed provide. Fluffy appeared and the bird understood and hopped onto her wings and off they went to catch up with the triangle of migrating screaming piha songbirds! The Amazon Rainforest was in four layers.

Some birds lived near the tops of the trees and remained there all year. The plants were all affected with the lack of rain and the beautiful tall red bark trees had their bark missing, leaving them burnt and bare open to even more damage.It was all too bad and Miss Daisy Weed needed rest to recover, she looked for her other half so they could rest, her other half looking for her hugged her and they promptly fell asleep. Elfvil woke them as he pranced around, dancing and playing his flute, he appeared so happy to see the two identical Miss Daisy Weeds. They followed Elfvil to his elf ring. It was so magical; elf fruit hanging from colored threads, mats and trays made of marshmallows and toadstools. Some insects walked around with toadstool trays on their backs, full of berries. Fruit juice mixed with morning dew was dripping constantly out of curled leaves that were positioned like funnels, catching the pink liquid from plants of deep green with pink and orange flowers and fruits. Small worms hung from the low branches of the trees. The large toadstools had pretty moist mosses to sit on. It was well received by these two daisies and after a quenching of their thirst, they fell promptly asleep once again. Miss Daisy Weed dreamt of her lovely life in the wild flower garden of Mr. Hill, her roots touching her wonderful Clover's roots and Horace laughing and all the plants and creatures happy in the safe, sunny and heavenly garden.Miss Daisy Weed dreamt of her view looking over the river that had been such an adventure, to find her scenic home and her best friend Daisy the cow.The two Miss Daisy Weeds awoke exactly at the same time, both their dreams had come true.

Chapter Five
Magical

Fluffy, now almost all purple, rested in the elves' ring camp, her wings stretched fully out under a large green plant that shaded her. She slept secure in the knowledge she had done as much as possible to help the planet, yet she also knew it was just a drop in the ocean, when she compared her help to what was needed to be done in the rainforest. She was never sure of how long she had lived in the forest, it seemed a long time and she certainly had many butterfly friends, some almost the color of the green plants, others that stood out with their shaded blue wings and also a similar one to the red admiral. She had spent a lot of time with the elves in their home, on many types of toadstools and swings made out of soft, flexible textured weeds that hung from the lower branches of some of the trees. Monkeys used them to swing, but also made perfect elf swings, they were covered in pretty colors of plants that were found on the borders of the rainforest. There were lots of unusual plants to be found in this vast Amazon Rainforest in South America.Fluffy was found by Tinkerbell when the elders sent her to the rainforest the first time. She needed help when her wings became tired and started to get dry too much with the heat. Fluffy was almost feeling despair, as there was so much to be done and she could not do all or even close to all without help. She was useful as a she could fly and therefore give news and comfort quickly around the forests but she needed someone to quickly move around the plants and trees skipping, hopping and running, zig zagging their way through the undergrowth.

This was impossible for Fluffy with her long wings and long body that had to crawl. The fairies and elves were so speedy and quite incredible, they flew, spotted problems and quickly dropped down to the ground to sort out whatever was wrong. Then up they went, even a bird could not depart from the earth and go straight upwards to tree tops to solve yet another problem. Yes, Fluffy so needed help when Tinkerbell came along and of course so did Tinkerbell need help, which she received from Fluffy. They were friends forever, but not only that, they were devoted like many others were to helping the Forests and their wonderful planet that they loved so very much and were so proud to have the privilege to live on. It was only a question of time until Fluffy would be working again with her fairies and elves, she waited and rested.She slept soundly and although she was in the elves' ring a sprinkling of fairy dust scattered over her. She looked up in surprise but was only in time to see Tinkerbell flying higher than the trees and heading for the blue of the morning sky. Fluffy fell into a very deep sleep under the large green plant.

Chapter Six
Fairy Counseling

The fairies flew swiftly around Miss Daisy Weed's garden, they were dropping lettuce leaves off with very small writing on, inviting all flowers and creatures who felt affected by the recent disaster to fairy counseling. This would be held, in a short while, at the fairy ring.

Miss Daisy Weed, although she loved her home in the soil in Mr. Hill's garden with her best friend Clover as her neighbor, had felt extremely sad. She could not quite understand why Kerry hated her and had trampled her almost to eternity, nor did she comprehend the earth turning over, or worse, Stanley who halved her with his spade. Why?

Miss Daisy Weed's other half was equally sad, although she loved her new home with the scenic view and her new best friend Daisy, but why did she go through so much pain and why did she want to be more than just be happy in Mr. Hill's garden. Why?

Clover, whose roots had not healed, felt sad that he was not the strong head of his family anymore, as his roots hurt and were very unpredictable, giving him pain when he had no explanation. Why?

Bee did not want to stay in with the workers in the hive, nor did he want to go out, he hated small spaces and was scared when he flew out into the open air, with the fear of small spaces. Why?

Red cried in the weeds and decided not to tell anyone about his sadness. He had looked down on the disaster and saw his many friends virtually buried alive, yet he could not help them and also discovered if he poured his heart out to his friends, they appeared not to listen, yet instead started to tell him of their troubles. Why?

Lily loved her new pond and the stream through her new garden home, but she missed the big pond in the parkland. Yet, she had more friends here and all the familiar goldfish with their siblings. Why?
Horace, poor Horace, he found it so hard to laugh, yet a while back he found it so hard not to laugh. Why?
Heather kept in touch with, lucky white heather in the cottage where Ginger the cat lived in luxury, after the lottery win. Yet for some strange reason, although so much more furniture and new cat baskets, Ginger and his owner were not happy. Why?
Goldie loved his family, he was proud of his pretty wife and their three little ones, yet he felt tired and fed up swimming around the pond. He even felt annoyed with his mother, as she swam close to him. Why?
Buster loved his walks with Sir Arthur or Johnny Brown, yet the lamp posts that he so enjoyed sniffing and the mystery of which dog had left the highest and strongest, smelling urine, seemed to be confusing. He dragged on his leash lamp post to lamp post, yet each time he tried to relieve himself on the smelly post he failed. Johnny Brown, as normal, had other more pressing things on his mind, so he never noticed poor Buster's failed attempts, at emptying his full bladder. Sir Arthur never missed anything, even after he had emptied half the decanter and so he was concerned when he saw poor Buster struggling with his favorite pastime. So an appointment was made at the vet's 9 am, Saturday morning. Buster however, emptied every drop of his full bladder on Lucy's gate and would, if he could, have emptied it on her, he knew. Why?

Lucy still did not like very much and the list was getting longer, bikes, spiders, dogs, fridges, Sir Arthur and cooking chocolate, she knew why!Sally never wanted to see Kerry again, or bright red lipstick, she knew why! Mr. Hill just wanted peace and to be left alone by all. He just wanted more plants, a bigger pond and to sit in his wonderful garden, watching the birds, bees and butterflies, smelling the gorgeous aroma and simply enjoying nature. He fitted a bigger lock on his gate, switched the doorbell off at 6 pm and he knew why!

Sir Arthur decided not to get pulled into village life and certainly not into Lucy's mother's life. He also decided to distance himself and drink less whiskey. He bought a bottle of very grand cognac, he knew why!

Johnny Brown developed a twitch. The first time he noticed his twitch, was walking past a junior girls school. Johnny Brown felt doomed to the opposite sex, with his very angry red spots, a developing twitch and a track record for dating twelve-year-olds. He had wrote another application to a large shipping company, to work on one of their many cruise ships. This time he posted the application, he knew why!

Jane was just sweet Jane, who enjoyed studying and reading, especially quiet places like libraries, she wore brown rimmed spectacles, pleated tweed skirt and put her hair in a bun, she knew why!

Kerry blamed everything on Miss Daisy Weed, she just never seemed to move on from the day she sat with Jane in the old lily pond, declaring her love and pulling petals off Daisy heads. The last petal should have read "he loves me" instead of "he loves me not." She felt so angry all the time, with everyone and especially daisies, she knew why!

The flowers and creatures could hardly wait for the fairy counseling, so when a little while later, a notice was placed at the entrance to fairy ring, showing opening time, "In a little while." There was a lot of excitement. There were mushrooms in rows and somehow all the flowers and creatures needing counseling were sitting under each mushroom, no one queried how suddenly they were there and seated with the stem of the mushroom as a back rest. It was so incredibly relaxing with the shade of the mushroom and soft fairy music in the background.

Poor Red cried, as he relaxed and was able to express his sadness at the recent disaster, seeing his friends struggle as the earth fell on them, burying some alive. He spoke with sobs as he recalled how tired he was as he flew to the lily pond for help and how his damaged right wing hurt. "No one would listen." He gulped.

Fairy Jessebell listened then took him to her foxglove, where he fell promptly asleep. Jessebell massaged his wings and spoke so gently to him, she explained how brave he had been, that he had not turned away, he had helped even though he was not well himself. Jessebell explained how not always do we get recognition for what we do and at times that includes the lack of anyone to listen when we hurt so much. Each flower, plant and creature on our planet has gone through so very much and so when sad things happen we find it brings out more conversations from others of their own sadness.

Red asked what should I do to feel better. Jessebell continued, when you flew to get help for your struggling friends and when you listened to Bee in the weeds about his recent dreadful near to death experience, both were important. One was more urgent at the time, but when you were in the weeds, you then had time to listen. What you are suffering from is an unnecessary conscience. Jessebell continued to explain to poor Red, how these things, thankfully do not happen too often, so how can any of us know how to behave. We can only follow the good book that all on the planet know and that is to be good, caring, kind, honest but most of all show love and that is what you have done. Jessebell then waved her wand over Red the sleeping, dreamy butterfly.

Bee who did not want to be there was crying for his mother Queen Bee, who could not leave her hive. Jessebell wanted to cry with him as she realized this pretty little Bee had been trapped in a small space for quite some time and worse someone was not just holding him hostage but trying to kill him. It was truly remarkable that he had survived at all. She reached out and beckoned Bee to lie under her wing, where she tried to console him. How could anyone do this to such a harmless little bee, who never even attempted or thought about using his sting on them. She told him how brave he had been and so forgiving as not to retaliate with his sting. Bee was fast asleep under Jessebell's wing and she decided to keep watch on this little Bee, she would make him strong again.

Bee listened as he slept soundly to Jessebell suggesting a plan. She would take him out each day on her wing, first day a short safe journey and eventually building up to longer journeys and definitely keeping him out of small spaces.

Jessebell knew the small spaces, were going to be the hardest as they were everywhere and most tempting to young inquisitive bees. Bee still fast asleep was placed back under his mushroom of learning.Clover, who was so loving to all, felt guilty that he was taking up fairy Tinkerbell's time. He felt his appointment should have been given to a more deserving course. Clover quickly explained that he felt weak and not the strong Clover he had always been. His roots hurting were only part of his pain, the real pain he felt went much deeper than roots. Tinkerbell smoothed his cloves as Clover slept, she spoke softly and very slowly.

"You are a star in our garden and always have been and always will be, but sometimes accepting change makes you more understanding," she continued, "only when we go through something ourselves, do we truly understand." Clover listened to the caring fairy that sat close as he slept, every word seemed to hit the pain he felt and had been carrying for such a long time, or so it felt. Tinkerbell explained how the pain in his roots would eventually go, as although they had been damaged when he was pulled out of the ground and thrown through the air, they were not so bad as he thought and were already healing. She also explained how, although he felt weak and not as strong in the eyes of his siblings and friends, this was only his imagination. He was every bit the Clover he was and would be for a long time to come. Clover slept soundly.

Horace was determined to stay awake as he thought he had seen all his friends returned to their mushrooms asleep and he did not want to miss any part of his rehabilitation.

Horace was already asleep when Jessebell spoke to him.
"Why do you want to laugh?" she asked.
Horace replied instantly, because most things in life are better when you see the funny side of it and most things do have a funny side."So why can you not see the funny side of not laughing, but wanting to," Jessebell laughed a rather high-pitched laugh.Horace explained how his mother had arthritic legs and that he had to carry all her shopping and make extra webs, leaving no time to laugh."Oh I see Horace, so we only laugh, when we have time and life is easier," Jessebell said.Horace was startled as he expected sympathy, "But my mother," he declared.Jessebell continued, "Your mother is very old and indeed very lucky to have you and you Horace are lucky to have your mother. It is a privilege to look after someone, especially your mother, who has looked after you and brought you up to be happy and laugh." Horace thought for a while and was trying to think what to say as a reply, but somehow could not think of a thing, instead, got the giggles as he thought of the rather large moth he was delivering to his mother, he remembered how he had crawled all the way from his web with the moth wrapped delicately in web only to find when he arrived at his mother's that the blessed moth had flown off. He giggled and laughed and was placed under his mushroom. Heather was so happy normally hearing from lucky white heather, who used to travel with the gypsies but now lived in a cottage with Ginger the cat and his owner Freddie. They had won the lottery because of lucky white heather, but strangely they were not so happy as they had been before. Tinkerbell explained that she should not be sad about Ginger and his owner's sadness.
They will learn money does not make you happy but used correctly they will both become happier.

We should not expect to be kind just when there are disasters, kindness comes in all different ways and some living creature on our planet will need our help every moment we are alive. We need always to reach out to help and show kindness. She continued, Ginger is a good cat and he would share his baskets if another animal came along, Freddie is a little different and is set in his ways, he does not want to share his money, so it sits in a bank and under the cushion of his armchair. He hates spending anything over his pension and so apart from a basket and new chair, his life is much the same as before, only he is depressed as he feels sad knowing he is wrong not to share and that he will die soon without spending and sharing his good fortune. His excuse: he may need it. Heather shook her mop of purple and the fairy smiled as she returned her under the mushroom.Goldie just could not wait, he gulped and spluttered, "I love my pretty wife and three babies and I love my mother," he continued without taking a breath of air, "I need space to swim, I am a drowning fish in a small pond, my mother is everywhere." Jessebell laughed at this cute little goldfish. "Oh well Goldie this problem is solved," and she pointed her wand, beckoning him to look. Goldie who believed he somehow was not under the mushroom but in the pond, jumped out of the water and looked to where the fairy's wand pointed. It took less than a glance to delight Goldie who spotted Mr. Hill with some workmen, measuring up for a bigger pond. Goldie dropped back into the imaginary pool as he was placed back under his mushroom.
Three elders came and transported all who had counseling back to their homes, all that was left were the two Miss Daisy Weeds.

Chapter Seven
The Importance of Being Miss Daisy Weeds

The two Miss Daisy Weeds appeared transfixed, their eyes looked almost in a hypnotic state as they stared directly ahead, not noticing the absence of their friends who were now all safely home.Snowbell was not known to many, she was a fairy elder who did a lot of work elsewhere and very few knew of her, and even the ones who did certainly could not say what she did, only that she was a wonderful fairy elder.
Snowbell loved her life and for quite a long time she roamed the woods and forests talking to trees and animals and all living creatures, she was so happy the radiance in her shone for a very long distance like the moon on a special fairy night. Snowbell was precious, in fact often she was called Precious Snowbell. Snowbell now stood in the front of the counseling room looking directly at the two Miss Daisy Weeds. Snowbell spoke softly and occasionally looked at her notes written in fairy ink on a very large lettuce leaf. "So Miss Daisy Weed you have been very sad and confused by the anger and pain that has been bestowed on you by others." The daisies noticed that she spoke to them as one. They knew not to reply to Snowbell and could not have done so even if they chose as they were held by her every word. Snowbell continued after another quick glance at her lettuce leaf for notes and also after a further document was handed to her from Maribell. "I believe you were confused a long time ago when you were almost still a bud and lived beside our honorable Clover.

You appeared to be having a battle within yourself, wanting to stay rooted beside Clover and your many friends and be contented and yet wanting to leave and see what life had in stow for you." She flapped her wing which had somehow got caught under a bit of twig, once her wing took its correct place Snowbell took on a more radiant role, she was soul inspiring, so pure and perfect, in her pink and lilac colors. She coughed a little screechy noise and continued, "Miss Daisy Weed you are sad that Kerry stamped on you in her anger, when you had not done anything at all to upset her and saddened that although the earth moved affecting you and all your friends, it appears it is what the child Stanley did to you with his spade." She quickly wiped a tear away, but one escaped and fairy Marinerbell rushed to catch it in a foxglove. Snowbell composed herself and continued, "The earth moving was fate, although brought about from material desires that affect the earth and our planet, what happened when Kerry and Stanley used their anger in a destructive way is out of our hands. We can only pray to our creator of the universe to correct or help us to understand and continue our existence in a better way, a more important way."

"You were one Miss Daisy Weed with longings and what happened to you is similar to what Horace the spider mentioned, in his humorous innocence, that you had been cloned," she continued, "it was in some way a remarkable solution to the battle you had going on in side of you, which had at many times, placed you in conflicting thoughts." Snowbell sat silent for a little while and then spoke again, "One part of you, Miss Daisy Weed, seemed more content and the other half appeared discontented."

She yawned and smiled, almost a laugh escaped, then continued again, "This however, was not quite right, as both halves are more content in many ways and both halves also want a little adventure, what is different is you are older and have responsibilities, so have others to consider." Tinkerbell who was in the background seemed extremely busy sorting out lettuce leaves with fairy notes on. She flew swiftly to Snowbell and handed her quite a few lettuce leaves, Snowbell glanced through these leaves and handed Tinkerbell a few back as she felt they did not apply to the present situation. The silence appeared to go on for a while and one of the elders brought Snowbell some dew drops to refresh her.
"To make this simple! The two Miss Daisy Weeds will remain in Mr. Hill's garden and in the scenic home, but you also will travel and work," she appeared to sneeze and giggle then continued with a huge smile on her most beautiful and perfect face, "you have been trained by Tinkerbell and Fluffy and met other workers in forests like Elfvil, you have experience that can not only help others but train others." Snowbell took on a more serious note as she continued a little faster, "You have done well, bringing out the good and fighting against the bad, yet still showing to all how alive you are."

Snowbell retired behind a very large fat stem of a mushroom, all that could be seen was her incredible pink shaded wings sticking out one at each side of the stem of the mushroom.
Strange noises came from where she hid herself, a little gargled gasp and then a humming noise in one key. Then she turned and beamed as she quickly finished her speech of instruction, "You will leave in a while and you will work very hard, as you have done before, at times you will be two Miss Daisy Weeds and other times you will be one, I trust you will accomplish your task and return to your life safely!"
The two totally confused Miss Daisy Weeds could only wonder as somehow they knew not to ask any details, they knew all would be revealed. They slept soundly, Miss Daisy Weed beside her lovely adorable friend Clover and Miss Daisy Weed beside her lovely adorable friend Daisy the Cow, but which Miss Daisy Weed was where?

Chapter Eight
When Two Become One

Fluffy, looking more blue than her original color of purple, seemed very agitated; she had just landed complete with the two Miss Daisy Weeds. They were sleepy, or so Fluffy thought. In truth they were excited. They both had no idea where they were or how they had got there, apart from a wonderful flight on Fluffy the butterfly's wings. Perhaps they were in the Amazon Rainforest but no matter how much or how hard they tried, they did not recognize their whereabouts. They could be anywhere in the world, apart from Mr. Hill's garden, Farmer Adam's field, and the majestic and magical Amazon Rainforest as they had been nowhere else. In truth, Miss Daisy Weed had been born in a different place but she was just a bud and it was too long ago to remember much about it.

A bright orange light shone from the ground near the base of a huge red bark tree. There, knelt down, wand lying on the ground was Snowbell, she was frantically digging with her hands and appeared to be making a very high pitched disturbing screech. "Help me please," she called out to the daisies who felt astonished, at how suddenly they could be beside her. "What is it?" they asked in unison. Snowbell did not look up but indicated at the terrified dog in front of her, her front right leg caught in a trap. It was a horrible, rusted animal trap. Snowbell had no idea what the trap had been used for. It had been hidden by the bracken and roots of the tree. The dog explained that she was with a pack of dogs looking for food as they had no homes since there had been loud bangs in their territory.

After the destruction of their homes and deaths of their owners, they had created a pack. They hunted together and slept together for warmth as the nights were extremely cold. They had tried food banks but they were sent away as hungry as they had arrived. Simona was the name of this poor injured and very frightened animal. Two fairies and three elves arrived after what seemed a long time later, the two daisies were stroking Simona's head with their petals. Snowbell kept trying to hit a certain high note, each time she missed she smiled, coughed, and tried again. It was after her fifth attempt that Snowbell hit the correct note required, this was such a relief not only to the daisies but to poor Simona, who decided she was steadily going barking mad. Snowbell was unperturbed and kept on humming. The extra magical help from the unknown fairies and elves, was all that was needed and suddenly a loud noise from the old rusted spring that held the trap in place around Simona's leg snapped open, enabling Snowbell to lift the dogs leg out and quickly wrap it in fresh garlands and herbs to heal it. The astonished dog had believed her life was over as she had been trapped there for several days and nights. Had it not been for her loyal friends in her pack, bringing her scraps and licking her distressed face, she would have given up long ago. Simona looked down at the daisies and Snowbell who was helping her and tried with all her might to smile a thank you. Simona was still not sure, if she was alive or dead as it was a lot to comprehend. Less than three months ago all Simona had to bark about was the fact that her owners put her last to be fed, they had a large family of children and grandchildren so often Simona thought there would be no food left for her but there always was. What she would give to be curled up in front of the fire on her favorite rug.

She promised herself, if she recovered, never everto grumble again or even bark.In the distance they all could hear the terrifying bangs, that Simona had spoken of with such fear in her eyes, they made the earth tremor and Miss Daisy Weed remembered the dreadful tremor in Mr. Hill's garden and all the damage it had done. Somehow this appeared to be on a much larger scale, as although where they were at present, nursing Simona, there were very little trees and plants, just lots of rubble where homes had been and all that remained of most was cement steps leading up or down to rubble. On the surface was broken glass and broken household furniture, even the window frames were broken and mainly covered in rubble. It was so sad watching the pack of dogs, trying to walk over this dangerous rubble. Some had badly cut paws and some that had splinters of glass still in their paws limped. Some lay trying to bite and lick their injuries, to get relief from the pain.

The pack of dogs kept circling the two daisies and Snowbell, but it was Simona their friend that concerned them far more than their own pain or these helpful strangers. Snowbell worked her magic on as many dogs as she could, cleaning and bathing their injuries, for fear of poison setting in. This was also the worry with Simona's leg, as the snare was extremely dirty and rusty, also she was starving and had been for a long time, so she had little flesh on her to fight any infection. Snowbell flew suddenly straight up and away, she sat on a branch, at the top of a very tall tree. She sighed and yawned, "What should I do?" she asked the tree.

The tree shook from top to root and when it eventually went still, Snowbell could see how part of the tree had been blown away and a lot of the bark had gone, "Oh what happened to you?" she asked as a sob escaped her. The poor tree pointed to where the bangs came from. He told her how he was once a proud tree in a row of trees, with flowers at the base, very pale lilac and pink, he explained in detail. "I was so very proud, then there was not just one, but several very large explosions, I lost a lot of branches as something hit my trunk, I thought my roots would come out of the ground, but somehow I managed to survive," he paused, "only two of the other trees that stood in the same row remain, but they are weaker than me and I am struggling, another explosion and I will surely fall." Snowbell changing the subject for fear they would both start to cry and be heard a very long way off, asked if he knew where she could get food and water for these poor wild dogs. The tree, which Snowbell had decided to call Adam, indicated that he could feel a spring running constantly over and around his roots, also he continued, "I do believe I get fruit on my branches." Snowbell grinned in satisfaction at her clever choice of names for this fruitful wonder! All she had to do was get some good wizard, then job down.Snowbell flew back to where Simona lay panting for breath, she sat down beside her and sung a rather high and certainly off-key tune. The two Miss Daisy Weeds, for now they were certainly two, had quite different ideas about this dreadful screeching Snowbell appeared to think was consoling. Miss Daisy Weed thought it clearly torture to keep the dog awake and prevent it slipping into some coma, the other Miss Daisy Weed thought she was probably attempting to contact some very powerful wizard and no sooner had shethought this than a triangle of blue and green light appeared.

It seemed to come from the sky and head to earth and appeared to be made up of particles of dust like matter. As it hit the ground the form of Manszard became clear. Few had ever seen Manszard, but most fairies and elves knew him to be a very powerful wizard, the best in his kingdom. Only a few wizards had more power and yet it was always the name Manszard all were told of. If the wind blew suddenly, the fairy elders would say that's Manszard, if elves were naughty, their elders would say, Manszard will turn you into a toad.

Manszard listened as Snowbell finished her dreadful off-key tune and then put his head down as Snowbell spoke of what was happening and how the poor dogs were starving.

"The tree…" she wept but could not quite finish and flew off to hide behind the tree close to where poor Simona yelped and fought for air. Snowbell gave vent to her sadness and wept long and hard. The two daisies, turned their petals up, to make cups to catch these precious tears. The two Miss Daisy Weeds were fearing their cups would overflow with Snowbell's tears when suddenly she stopped and took the two daisies carefully to Simona and tipped the daisy cups carefully into Simona's mouth. Simona drank with satisfaction and fell peacefully into a sound and dreamy sleep, she was back with her parents in front of the fire on her favorite rug.

Chapter Nine
Miss Daisy Weeds, Fairies, Elves and a Wizard

The fairies and elves sat in a circle awaiting Manszard the wizard. The two daisies sat with their backs resting on a broken cider bottle, they were all tired as they had helped Snowbell with the pack of injured dogs; massaging, comforting and promising fruitful food. Dogs do eat fruit if they are hungry, Snowbell explained to the leader of the pack, who said they were all leaving shortly to catch a train or look around a station in hope of scraps, the train journey seemingly was a regular journey the dogs took to keep warm.Manszard arrived in similar power as before, as the beam of blue and green in a triangle shape approached the earth, he lifted his arms in a jester for all to sit but Snowbell who was already sitting appeared to be plating her hair and was very distant to Manszard's dramatic jests. Seeing Manszard in his stunning gold and purple gown was more than enough for poor distressed Snowbell, who just wanted a quick solution to these starving and in pain dogs.

Manszard would help but in return he wanted Mr. Hill's Garden and all what lived there. Snowbell who had almost completed her plat and was about to tie a strong grass she had found around the base to keep it firmly in place dropped the plat in shock of what she heard. The two Miss Daisy Weeds lost their confidence and yearning for adventure and clung to each other, their petals soft and still wet from Snowbell's tears. The unknown fairies stood strong, the elves laughed in the face of the wizard.

Snowbell was the first to speak, all she could ask was "Why?" The wizard laughed at her and all his now very alert, mixed audience, "I need a laboratory to do tests and I need all in the garden to do tests on." "But it's not possible," Snowbell gulped, "I asked you here today to help the poor injured and starving animals and now you are abusing the situation and wanting to hurt more innocent trees, plants and animals and fish," she gulped as she thought of the lily pond. Snowbell sounded incredibly strong and indeed powerful as she continued, "Besides there is no laboratory there so..."But she was not loud enough to finish as Manszard said, "Mr. Hill will go, he will be ill and I will have his conservatory, his daughter is already packing to go, do not question me, you silly little goody helpers," and with that he had gone in a puff of green light. Snowbell looked on in dismay and then commenced plating her hair once again. At least that dreadful tune had not commenced, the two daisies thought, and a few more thought that too. They would all sleep and on awaking would decide about the fruit tree and the spring. Snowbell said her goodbyes and fell promptly asleep, the two daisies looked on in disbelief. The elves and the fairies seemed to be playing some game of catching and tickling dragonflies, the elves appeared to be bored with this whimsical fairy pastime and soon flew off, although they were not far away from this little mixed tribe, who desperately needed their help.Manszard appeared at daybreak. Snowbell sat on a large green palm plant, she was singing a fairy song and appeared to also be eating red and black berries. Snowbell stopped singing occasionally in the middle of an extremely high note, munched on her delicious berries, and then continued from where she had stopped on exactly the very high note.

Manszard appeared angry at the lack of attention he received and threw some fairy wands, which he had obtained through trickery, into the air. This certainly did the trick, as far as Manszard was concerned, as he watched the frightened little group jump as blue, green and orange lights shot into the air. He laughed a deep grunted laugh and indicated to the elves who appeared to be watching him from a distance, half hidden by the undergrowth where they took turns watching and sleeping, for fear of the wizard's return.Snowbell licked her lips and drank some dew drops, then with a special leaf she had found, wiped her rather angelic face. Manszard was angry once again as he noticed the relaxed Snowbell, "Have you thought any more of my remarkable and kind offer," he asked in annoyance to this obviously disinterested fairy."NO," replied Snowbell, and although she spoke softly, the word no shook the earth and everything on it including Manszard, who quickly left the ground as the powerful thunder of her word seemed to echo on and on. Simona who had been relaxing after the best sleep she had known in a long time, lifted her head and grinned at this clever and yet so strong little fairy. Snowbell flew to her side and stroked the dark brown hair of this part greyhound and part terrier dog, she offered her some berries and some water which she had left lying beside the dog for when she woke. Simona ate and drank gratefully.

"No," mimicked Manszard, "no," he repeated, enraged by all and everything. Manszard flew to where the poor injured Simona lay. "I will turn this dog into a snake, I may also put it back into the trap."

"No," mimicked Manszard, "no," he repeated, enraged by all and everything. Manszard flew to where the poor injured Simona lay. "I will turn this dog into a snake, I may also put it back into the trap." At this, a loud noise was heard from where the elves were; they had placed a broken twig into the rusted trap and the trap had snapped shut. Manszard continued, "Then she will be turned into a snake." At this the wizard produced three more fairy wands and threw them into the air casting a spell on poor frightened Simona, who certainly did not want to be a snake. "Jessrrrgersnakkk," he screamed at Simona, but to everyone's surprise, apart from Snowbell's there appeared to be not a thing happening. Snowbell had previously cast spells on all fairy wands that Manszard had in his possession. So, without knowing what the spells on these stolen fairy wands were reset to, all were safe from harm, especially poor Simona who appeared delighted with her escape from turning into a reptile. Manszard had long since gone and it had been a very hard day for all, as they had moved swiftly around the rubble that had once been home to so many animals and humans. A lot of birds had left when the explosions had started but they were the lucky ones. There were campsites of humans and animals but they were by no means adequate; children and animals searched the rubble to find food, or something to lie on to remind them of their past comforts. The two Miss Daisy Weeds stayed mainly around the plants and trees and the very few flowers that were left, struggling to grow from the rubble.

The two Miss Daisy Weeds knew this experience personally and comforted their fellow plants, telling them of new and brighter tomorrows. Hope and never give up hope, they told to as many almost-destroyed plants that were willing to listen. They spoke of their own injuries and how the fairies helped them, the plants no matter how damaged they were seemed to look brighter and a little more alive. The two daisies eventually after such a long time met back at what they now called the elves' camp, their petals ached with all the healing they had given, massaging the weary dried and forgotten flowers and small plants. Snowbell was still working her magic on the few remaining trees and dropping fairy dust on the children who searched the rubble, who quickly after her fairy dust had scattered, seemed to find something, a loaf of bread still in a plastic wrapper, still fresh to eat, as it was under the rubble with just the end bit of plastic sticking out. The lucky child ran at speed back to his mother, who wept with joy at such an offering. She picked her son up and kissed him swinging him around in her arms, as she looked up to the sky and thanked God. A dog found a tin of sardines which, although had been previously opened and eaten in haste, still had a sardine in the corner of the tin covered in sunflower oil. The dog his tongue searching the inside of the tin almost jumped for joy as he chewed carefully this delicious sardine, in his favorite oil. Snowbell was flying quite low to the ground and what she spotted disturbed her, partly with fear and partly with excitement. She decided to fly around again to make sure what she had seen was correct and not just a glove sticking out from the rubble.

It was obvious by the type of rubble that it had been a home as there appeared to be part of a cot, cooking pans, an upturned cooker, curtains and some type of matching seating which was oddly sitting upright. It looked so sad and deserted, what had once been some ones cherished home. Snowbell swooped down almost afraid of what she might or might not discover. She landed right beside what did turn out to be a white baby's or small child's glove. She touched the glove very gently, an empty cola can lying close rolled away as the small child trapped beneath the rubble sensed something magical, he moved his tired and almost numb fingers inside the warm knitted glove, his mother had placed on his hands, to protect him from the cold night air. Snowbell stroked the hand in comfort and as she flew off to get help, the frightened almost dehydrated child, somehow knew to trust whatever was so powerful above the surface. Snowbell circled around making each circle bigger than the last, this way she would not miss anything. Then suddenly she spotted on a high rubble across, a man and woman crying, looking up to the heavens for help from their pain and suffering, of loss of their eight-month son Thialak. The lady who cried was in the arms of her husband, who could not console his wife as he himself was beyond consoling. The lady fell into what appeared to be a sleep, she had cried for her son and her hands bled as she frantically searched and moved as much rubble as she could over the days that followed the blast that had destroyed their world. The sleep appeared to be exhaustion and escape from such pain, Thialak was their only child and now he had gone. The lady dreamed of a white glove sticking out from the rubble, close to a cola can.

She woke with a jump of alertness and felt she had slept for hours. Her husband was disappointed as he wanted his wife to sleep and feel better but she had barely closed her eyes and had awoken with such a jump. "What is it?" he asked, yet feared his all too obvious question could bring about even more tears and anguish. Instead, she smiled. He thought she must be still half asleep and not remembering the loss of their devoted son. Snowbell watched as the parents of baby Thialak ran down the rubble, her husband who desperately wanted to believe his wife's dream, fearing it could just be wish full hope playing tricks but somehow, he could neither stop his wife's hope nor his own."Tell me what are we looking for and where? " he asked his wife, as his words came out jumbled.

"A cola can!"

Snowbell decided to help this desperate couple find their baby, as she could hear the baby gasping for air. Snowbell dropped some bright purple fairy dust where the cola can lay beside the tiny, now totally numb, hand. The couple who were already running frantically did not stop to query this purple dust, they ran with speed like the wind to the very spot shown in the mother's dream; the empty cola can and there to both their amazement was baby Thialak's glove. The mother tenderly felt her babies hand in the white knitted glove. The hand felt so cold and yet, her hope for her baby to be alive was greater than anything she had ever known in her life. Her husband gently removed stone by stone, he did not stop when he arrived at a boulder which would take at least two strong men to remove, somehow he managed to lift it straight up and off without harming his little one. His wife bent into the tomb where Thialak had lain protected by this gigantic stone boulder, covered with surface rubble.

She reached out her arms and picked out her baby who was covered in grey dust and cement. At first, the couple who were almost stunned into silence and stared in wonder and disbelief. The baby being back in his mother's arms moved slightly, making the smallest of cries and yet there was no doubt their baby Thialak had survived such an ordeal and for such a long time. The parents looked to the heavens and thanked God, they were not totally sure what they saw but it certainly was pink and had wings. Snowbell flew, almost blinded by her tears as she queried why anyone on such a beautiful planet would do this, she just could not comprehend. She would compose herself before she returned to the elves' ring. Snowbell sat near the top branches of a red bark tree, her tears were uncontrollable. She had her face close to the leaves, which appeared to be catching her tears. Tears dropped from one leaf to the next making their way to the lower branch, where she had lain her wand, for safe keeping. As the first tear drop reached the magical fairy wand, a noise like thunder rattled in the sky above the tree top. Snowbell jumped with fright as her mind was focused on the cruel destruction that was affecting so much of the planet and as far as Snowbell could understand, for no reason. As she looked up to the sky she was just in time to see Manszard flying at speed and circling the tree top where she sat weeping and praying for fairy help. At the same time the noise of thunder had rang where all the fairies and Miss Daisy Weed lived with all their other friends. Snowbell's tear had landed on her fairy wand and what happened next was not just incredible but a wonderful display of color set to fairy music. As Snowbell's tear landed on the wand it shot at speed in shocking shades of pink, lilac and orange up and around following the rather stunned and bewildered wizard.

As each of Snowbell's teardrop followed the first, they took on a speed never seen by fairies, elves and certainly not wizards. Manszard, his wings quickly tiring, desperately tried to fly faster out of reach of Snowbell's tears that were closing in on him. At the same time as this strange yet brilliant display of fairy tears was happening, soft fairy music could be heard. The music appeared to get louder as it closed in on the panic-stricken wizard and as the first tear hit Manszard it seemed to reach quite a volume. The tear stopped the wizard in mid-flight and he struggled with what appeared to be his conscience. Snowbell watched as the wizard's body took on a crumpled withered appearance, then he appeared to strengthen and straightened himself just in time for the next tear drop to hit him and so it went on until everyone of Snowbell's tears had hit his conscience. Three unknown training wizards flew to the stumbling-out-of-the-sky Manszard and rescued him. Manszard's wings lay closed against his shaken body, he could not comprehend how such power could come from a little fairy, he had never seen anything even close to this display of conscience tapping. He would think about revenge later, meanwhile, he wanted to hide away and recover.Snowbell neatly unfolded the first leaf that had caught her tear and straightened out the leaves she had been sitting on and flew off.

Chapter Ten
Blossom Where I Am Planted

Two little tired Miss Daisy Weeds sat in the elves' ring camp awaiting the return of Snowbell. They had held each other tight, their petals wrapped around each other's stem for comfort as they watched the most powerful display of fairy magic they were ever likely to see. As the wizard had been clearly seen being helped across the night sky by his wizard helpers. The two daisies had rejoiced but had stopped their inner satisfaction for fear they could be punished, so instead they prayed for the soul of Manszard and his helpers.

Elfvil had returned a while back with Fluffy, who had collected him from where the blasts destroying this unfortunate part of the planet came from. Elfvil had not had time to escape the last blast completely and a sticky type of substance had attached to his wings making it extremely hard to fly home. Psychic Fluffy had sensed Elfvil was struggling and flew bravely close to where the blasts could be heard, without fear for her own life. She was truly remarkable but now she slept safely out of sight behind Elfvil's personal mushroom, dreaming to be safely home with the elves in the Amazon Rainforest. Snowbell arrived bearing lots of fresh berries and trailing some never-seen-before fruit. Before she greeted the wide eyed daisies, she flew to where Simona lay, also eagerly awaiting Snowbell's return. Snowbell fed Simona juice and fruit and checked the injured leg for infection. After a full and satisfactory examination, she then placed fresh healing leaves and herbs around a recovering Simona, who could hear her faithful friends in the distance calling for her.

Simona feeling content, safe and warm and slept soundly rolled in a comfortable ball, a position she could not have managed a while ago. Even her tail was wanting to wag, she could not wait to return to her friends and hopefully a new good life one day, meanwhile, she was grateful for life and her caring new friends. Snowbell, with juice from the nutritious red berries dripping off her face, seemed very busy talking to a rather colorful bird. She then climbed into the bird's nest which was on a lower branch of a tree hanging over the elves' camp, the bird flew off happy to have helped and Snowbell, licking her lips, fell promptly asleep. The two Miss Daisy Weeds looked on amazed and also fell asleep. Looking down on this quiet little camp was a nostalgic wonder of total peace governed and lead by love. Elfvil had work to do and extremely private work, he looked cautiously at Snowbell sleeping as he tip toed out of the camp and then took flight, steering at speed in the early morning light in the direction of the wizard's black tower. The tower moved constantly as it moved with the wind, so finding it could be hard even on a calm day. Elfvil was very different to Snowbell, who innocently went about her life and work, only knowing and believing in good and avoiding bad. Elfvil, however good he had become after being tried for stealing and selling fairy wands to the wizard's for wizardry, still knew it was a corrupt world and sometimes to deliver good you had to deal with bad. Manszard's fairy wands that had a spell put on them so he could not use them was very clever and Elfvil applauded Snowbell for such a genius solution. However, it just made Manszard more angry and more determined to own Mr. Hill's garden. So Elfvil went to sell and make deals with some spare fairy wands. All fairies were good so their wands were extremely powerful. Elf wands or magic was not as powerful, as they could be and mostly were very mischievous.

All wizards were powerful but because they were all bad their power came from the use of fairies' wands and spells and elves' not so good power. They claimed or stole anything they could but they could easily have their power taken away temporarily by pure good fairy spells. The latter is what had just happened to Manszard, when Snowbell's pure tears of feelings and love had dropped from her eyes and chased Manszard through the sky, destroying his stolen power and stopping his evil intentions. Snowbell always had known good would overpower evil and yet the wizards appeared not to realize that evil would not win over good. Elfvil just wanted to negotiate the best deal, to get Manszard to leave his desire of obtaining Mr. Hill's garden and to please the fairies and feed proud of himself.Elfvil, who had seen the black tower through the clouds, flew direct to an open window high up the tower. He felt as if he was being sucked at force through the open window and along a dark and damp smelling corridor that Elfvil feared was endless. Suddenly, he was stopped and dragged head first backwards then sideways into and an even darker room. Fumes from the corner of the room hurt his eyes and made him feel sick. Elfvil, fearing he would never see light of day ever again, felt panic run through every part of his body. He reached his arms out into the darkness and then to his amazement the darkness lifted to the top of the room. And there in the corner of the room where the fumes came from, was a very frail Manszard leaning on what appeared to be a cauldron. The fumes were coming from whatever concoction in the cauldron Manszard appeared to be inhaling as if it was the last air on the planet. He also looked like a withered wizard, bent and frail, his body more like bones that had no flesh on, under his black trailing-the-ground gown. "I have been expecting you."Elfvil flinched and felt glued to the spot.

Manszard laughed. "Oh, did you expect to fly off when you choose to, well I don't think so, you stupid elf," he sneered, as Elfvil tried to conjure his magic to escape, but he could not move a finger let alone his wings, that were feeling heavier and heavier.Elfvil thought how Snowbell had spoken so bravely and so with the strongest voice he could find in him, looked at Manszard directly and said: "Oh-ho who is silly? Look at you, you are fragmented into fragments ha ha and by a little fairy, whereas I, an elf, appear not so silly as I have the fairies' spell to reverse your present situation, yet I cannot give it to you, as I am in your temporary spell." Manszard cursed Snowbell and the darkness which covered the top of the room dropped almost to the floor.Snowbell was sitting crossed legged eating a fruit stick, one of her favorites, as it reminded her of when she was younger. Fruit sticks were just a few different fruits on a stick and covered in honey and marshmallow. Snowbell found it comforting and it helped her to ponder over the day ahead. These delicious fruit sticks were given to Snowbell when the elders had sat late into the moonlight and taught Snowbell to thank the Almighty in the heavens, above the sky, for the universe and the planet they lived on. Then Snowbell would be asked to make three wishes after which a fruit stick was given. Snowbell felt some evil power and then the fruit stick seemed to lift out of her hand and into the air. At first the stick with the fruit circled, then the fruit left the stick and kept circling. As Snowbell looked, each bit of fruit had Manszard's evil face on it. Snowbell looked away and made a wish, a very good wish, as all the fruit seemed to dance in the air to fairy music and land one by one at a very surprised and rather confused Simona's paws.

Simona sniffed then after licking the first bit of fruit that tasted more like some special dog treat, ate every piece. Manszard who had used up his last ounce of power, slumped to the floor the darkness covering him and blending into his lifeless body.Elfvil spoke again, "Well I really must be on my way." The words spoken were not only for this deformed figure sprawled on the ground, but for Snowbell who was waiting to hear from him. Snowbell was not asleep merely dreaming when Elfvil left the camp in the early morning. Snowbell had communicated with her mind and senses with him and although Elfvil was not the best at mind communication, he still managed.Snowbell called to the two Miss Daisy Weeds, "Come I need you to help." And as the two Miss Daisy Weeds accepted this offer very readily, Snowbell proceeded to place them in a plant green leaf that she had made into a cone. The top had a strong weed threaded through the top with two loops. After securing the two smiling daisies, Snowbell then placed her arms through the loops. This made it easier to fly with the two Miss Daisy Weeds comfortably positioned like a satchel on her back. Snowbell, once she put her thoughts to a plan, was fast into action. They flew fast and direct to the wizard's black Tower and through the open window and along the dark and sinister corridor and quickly arrived where Manszard and Elfvil were. The room smelt unbearable and the two happy Miss Daisy Weeds suddenly felt quite ill.

Snowbell had created her own protection spell before she left and sprinkled the precious ointment on the daisies faces and then on Elfvil, who had already been sick several times already.

"Give me that," Manszard screamed, but Snowbell did not reply and merely trapped Manszard in spellbound mode. As she waved her wand, that the two daisies had kept safe between them as they flew, it was the third and most powerful wand that all fairy elders possessed and was mainly used for good. The cauldron lifted in the air turning upside down and then placed itself over Manszard's head.All Snowbell said, as she left the room with Elfvil who had suddenly been released from his paralyzed position, was, "Enjoy, Manszard."Instead of flying directly back to the elves' camp they landed where children and adults searched the rubble. The twobeautiful smiling Miss Daisy Weeds ran, or flew, to different directions. They were not sure, just suddenly they were in every place they wished to be. A small child engraved in dirt and dust, her feet bleeding from the tins and broken bottles she stood on, noticed the smiling Miss Daisy Weed. The child bent down and picked the smiling Miss Daisy Weed they looked directly into each other's face and then the child smelt and kissed Miss Daisy Weed. As Miss Daisy Weed moved to the next victim of these bombs that searched this large amount of rubble the small under nourished girl, she was a child again, her imagination lightening the load of these sad days. The two Miss Daisy Weeds could see each other as they greeted each child on this man-made heap of hope and torture to each unfortunate little soul. She watched a little boy run bare foot over the rubble, not noticing the pain as his feet cut on the dangerous carpet of open tins and broken glass, his hand held high holding his new found trophy of a half opened tin of beans which appeared to still contain some beans.

Miss Daisy thought of the wonderful wild flower garden she had been fortunate enough to live in and then suddenly a path of wild flowers covered the rubble. The child ran down, he began to dance as his feet felt like feathers on moss ground. Miss Daisy Weed's other half watched as two little boys tugged at a plastic bottle, Miss Daisy Weed wept as she thought of Daisy the cow with all her lovely fresh milk in the country field and the two starving little boys tugging at the almost-buried plastic bottle, hoping it contained some kind of liquid. Suddenly the bottle came out of the ground, the two little boys stared in amazement as they discovered it was a full bottle of milk. The little boys sat down on what they believed to be a field with daisies and a cow and drank the creamy milk between them. They were happy children again! The two Miss Daisy Weeds returned with Snowbell to the elves' camp. They were sad and confused, so much unnecessary sadness which neither made sense or had any reasonable explanation. Snowbell, realizing how sad the two Miss Daisy Weeds appeared to be, decided to show them something to cheer them up. Snowbell waited until all in the elves' camp had ate and drank and then gathered up the two sad daisies. They flew to where the children had been searching the rubble. Close to the rubble heap was a large camp with many tents, some just blankets looking like tents. It was becoming dark and lights shone from gaps in these man-made homes.

On closer inspection, as Snowbell dived close enough to glimpse in through the gaps of light, the two Miss Daisy Weeds smiled with delight as they saw the children they had helped wearing Daisy chains and small jars with daisies in water displayed on their treasured possessions.

Each tent had daisies somewhere, some in Daisy chains across the entrance and others around their necks and wrists. A little boy sat with his brother in the light of a candle, drawing on the back white page of a book they had found in the rubble. What they drew were two smiling Miss Daisy Weeds. When the tired fairy and two very tired but happy Miss Daisy Weeds arrived back at camp for the last time that night, Snowbell decided to speak and explain to them what they had seen."Your good wishes and thoughts were for others and they came true, they were not wishes for yourself, they were not selfish, they were pure and full of love, you have learnt so very much and now you must teach others what you now know." The two daisies fell asleep under the wings of Snowbell. Snowbell, her love pouring over for these lovely flower friends, allowed two tears to fall, one for each Miss Daisy Weed. Manszard's helpers arrived at the camp at first light. The three wizard's helpers stood angry, waiting for reaction to their arrival but the camp was still in silence as none but Snowbell was awake. She gently took her wings away from the sleeping daisies and sat up brushing her tangled pink hair. She had slept sound but her dreams had been restless. Snowbell knew it was not the end of Manszard and so she listened to these evil wizards.

"We want the potion for Manszard or he will damage all wings on elves and fairies, then he will live and cause evil to Mr. Hill's garden."

"Oh really," Snowbell replied to the red-faced wizard, "and how, may I ask, does he propose to do this when he can hardly move and is totally addicted to fairy potions?""He can take them or leave them," replied the same wizard, who appeared to be spokesman for the three wizards.
"Well, he needs a potion now, then he will not need any further ones," the wizard said, sounding a little stupid.
"How very sad for you all as you all look as if you have drunk and inhaled lots of fairy potions." Snowbell sneezed, waking up the two Miss Daisy Weeds and the rest of the camp. "I am sad for you all, but the best I can do is not give you any, therefore you have a small chance to get better, once you do, come look me up." Snowbell paused, then with a hidden giggle escaping, continued,
"Look me up." Snowbell handed the wizards a calling card. It read.

Fairy Snowbell
Fairy Glen
Mr. Hill's Garden
Fairies at the bottom of the Garden.

Chapter Eleven
Welcome Home, Miss Daisy Weeds

Snowbell had a few loose ends to finalize before she left the elves' camp, the first one was Simona. Simona was a lot stronger and appeared to want to run with her pack, she could hear her friends in the distance barking and howling but this morning was different. The pack of dogs had come very close to the elves' camp. Ever since Simona was found by Snowbell the pack of dogs never left Simona and although they realized she was ill and also that they themselves had to hunt, their loyalty for Simona never faltered. So, Simona could hear them at various times of each day in the distance as they went about their hard lives to survive. Today they barked and waited for Simona to join them. Snowbell was greatly troubled, as Simona would never keep up with the pack in her condition. She would never be fast enough to hunt or jump. So, Snowbell fed Simona and asked her to await her return before she decided to join her friends. Snowbell left the camp and flew at speed to the tent where baby Thialak was with his mother. Snowbell flew in through the gap and there was the mother nursing her beloved little baby boy. The baby screamed as he tried to sleep but his fears were embedded in him. His mother looked with sadness as she saw the trauma in her son's eyes. She was lost with how to console her frightened child. She rocked and rocked him and then with the help of Snowbell's magic wand, the mother and son fell fast asleep. The mother dreamt of her baby boy playing with a dog. The dog had beautiful kind eyes, the dog was Simona. Thialak and his mother awoke at the same time and began to get ready for the day.

Snowbell returned to the camp to find, not to her surprise, that Simona had gone to join her waiting friends.It had been a difficult decision for Simona, as her old pack friends were loyal, but so were these new wonderful friends. Without either of these packs of friends, Simona knew she would not be alive. She knew she had to leave one day to be with her own. She wished things could be different as she could not see how she could ever keep up with the pack. She limped to where the pack of dogs waited for her, the leader of the pack, came close to Simona licked her face and sniffed her injured leg. He knew it was impossible for poor injured Simona and so he beckoned her to return to the elves' camp.Simona ignored and knew her chances to survive were very low, but to stay at the elves' camp was also impossible, so she limped on, pain and weakness taking over with every agonizing step. Simona had almost lost sight of the fast-moving pack, although she could still hear them. It seemed like eternity to Simona as she gasped for air to keep her moving, in fact it was barely noon. Simona stopped where a lot of women appeared to be filling plastic containers with water from a parked truck containing a tank of water. Simona limped to the front of the queue, her legs shaking with the strain of the journey, she was desperate for water. A woman with a little baby boy strapped tightly to her back, walked out of the queue and moved to where Simona now lay panting and desperate for help. She stroked the frightened Simona, who with a dry tongue licked the lady's hand. The lady took out a piece of thin rope from her skirt pocket used to tie the tent's door, she placed it through the loop on Simona's worn collar. The child on the woman's back giggled as he looked with delight at his new best friend.

The woman filled her plastic bottle with water, made a cup with her hands to allow Simona to drink and then the three of them set off for home. Snowbell who had followed Simona all the way flying so close at times, she was sure Simona knew she was there, smiled as she watched the baby Thialak giggle with delight as Simona looked up at his new owners. She barked three thank you barks as Snowbell flew back to elves' camp.

The two Miss Daisy Weeds sat facing each other. "You must have been wishing for them again."

"I never had, I would not, that would be selfish."

"Then maybe you did not know you made a wish for legs."

Each Miss Daisy Weed accused the other, as they looked at their incredible legs. These were not Horace's spider legs, these were magnificent fairy legs, the best in the whole world as far as these two daisies were concerned. They decided to try to stand on them and found to their delight it was easy. When Snowbell arrived at the camp, she viewed two Miss Daisy Weeds playing leap frog over the toadstools, the elves looked on amazed at these flower fairies and they laughed as the happiness shining from their Daisy faces was infectious. Snowbell was neither surprised nor amazed but was so very happy for these two helpful and pure Miss Daisy Weeds who now had a very old wish granted. Snowbell, after watching the daisies play many games, chasing, hiding even a running race, decided time to step in and rescue them as daisies were not made for legs and they soon would find that out as their stems dried out and their petals.

As suddenly as their legs had come, they disappeared and Snowbell collected the daisies from where they now lay and took them under her wings. She then placed their stem in some water that she had ready for them in an upturned toadstool. They drank as much as was there but then were incredibly tired. Snowbell placed some soil in the toadstool and left them there with the moisture of the soil stopping their roots from drying. Tomorrow was a long journey home for these two Miss Daisy Weeds so sleep was the best remedy. Snowbell had yet another surprise in store for them, another old wish.

Fluffy had other work to do for the fairy elders and had left several days before, she was flying back to the Amazon Rainforest where she would meet fairy Tinkerbell and fairy Jessebell, she had said her good byes to the camp and she could not wait to go as it felt like going home. She was fully rested and ready to help the fairies with their new adventure. So, Snowbell had the journey back to Mr. Hill's garden totally her responsibility and she was already feeling tired. She looked at her wings that seemed quite heavy, she dusted them with a feather she found in the birds nest she used to sleep in, they still looked a little faded and felt heavy. When fairies were tired, mainly from mental concentration and communication, their wings would ache and feel heavy. Also, the color would look faded and they would feel as if they had flown many miles. Snowbell slept close to Elfvil as it was the last night for a while before they would see each other again and with Manszard's bad wizards' spells Snowbell felt sad leaving him, although she knew deep down, he would be more than capable to deal with Manszard. Elfvil sat on the other side of the toadstool Snowbell had lain under, she sang some fairy songs, ate some juicy berries Elfvil had given her, yawned and fell promptly asleep.

In fact, everyone in this paradise of elves, fairies and daisies fell asleep, no one kept watch other than the ruler of the universe, watching with satisfaction the purity of his creations. Snowbell awoke, said her fairy wishes, bathed in dew drops, combed her hair and placed a large shell in the side of her hair. She wanted to look nice for her return journey home. The Miss Daisy Weeds were still both asleep in the toadstool so instead of waking them, Snowbell used the toadstool like she had used the cone and then placed it on her back. She flew directly up from the elves' camp and without a glance back headed for home. Elfvil, instinctively feeling the emptiness in his heart as Snowbell left, sat upright gulping his tears for fear they would fall from his eyes. He looked down and there, almost hidden by the grasses, was a hair shell. Elfvil had many times seen Snowbell wearing two shells in her long hair, she had left one for Elfvil to deliver it one day to her and also to remind him, he is not alone. Elfvil smiled and pinned the shell to the top of his green tunic, elves always wore green sometimes with a red pom pom on the end of a green elf hat. They sometimes got mistaken for pixies, but this annoyed them as elves were incredibly clever, whereas pixies were not clever, they liked to laze around, they started lots of jobs and never finished one and made an incredible mess. Elfvil was good to them but mainly because he had no other choice. pixies would just appear behind toadstools in elf camps, they were smaller than elves and hard to spot, sometimes Elfvil was not sure how many pixies were in his camp but he could certainly smell them as they rarely washed. The shell safely pinned on, Elfvil was ready to commence the day.

Snowbell had communicated to him whilst he slept and first on her list was for him to clean the camp and then go to see baby Thialak and Simona and then drop an old wand off for Manszard, it had potions to help addictions of potions. Elfvil ate, instructed his elf helpers to clean camp and off he went to baby Thialak. He laughed with glee as he saw Simona lying under Thialak's crib on a rather thick and furry pink rug. Simona yawned and turned onto her back, a very contented position. He stroked Simona's head, she knew to be quiet but if she could, she would have purred with delight. She was one very happy dog and was ready to grow up with this wonderful baby boy who she loved as much as he loved her. Both had suffered and believed their life was over and yet somehow through the love of a fairy they had been given so much happiness.
Thialak's mother had prepared two small dishes of food, one for Thialak and the other for this wonderful dog that was now part of their family. Simona was re-christened Sim, as Thialak's first word spoken was Sim. Elfvil sat under a tree and communicated to Snowbell, telling her of the sight of happy Simona and his new family. Thialak's father had returned before Elfvil had left, he kissed his wife and then rushed to nurse his baby patting Simona with his other hand, the man looked up and thanked God. Elfvil told Snowbell this as well but Snowbell was so tired and hungry she could hardly show her pleasure at what she had just heard. Snowbell was on a treetop it swayed and bent over in the strong wind, that was relentless she had been flying against the gust most of the day.

The two Miss Daisy Weeds were awake, their heads sticking out of the curled toadstool they wriggled as suddenly there was lack of space in this toadstool and as they struggled to get their petals out to their surprise what sprung out either side of their heads was wings in startling pastel shades lilac and pinks, like fairy wings. The wings lay down the side of their stems like a moth's wings do, when they sleep. The wind gave one almighty powerful gust and Snowbell fell backwards with the weight of the daisies and due to tiredness as she had little strength left. This remarkable little fairy had forgotten about her own needs to stay healthy and had flown and worked beyond her body's strength. As Snowbell toppled backwards from the tree top, the two Miss Daisy Weeds fell out of the mushroom rucksack. As the gust of wind caught their new and beautiful wings, they became air born. They flew with speed that would have surprised Fluffy, who complimented herself on her speed, but this speed was to rescue Snowbell who was already nearing the last branch of this tall tree. The two air born flower fairies swooped under Snowbell then quickly gathered her up between their petals, which felt more like arms. They flew close to the tree top and sat on a safe strong branch, cuddling this wonderful little fairy who had given so much of herself to others. Snowbell gave in to this little rescue team, all she had strength left for was to point with her wand the direction home. The two Miss Daisy Weeds flew, their wings in perfect rhythm that never faltered, with Snowbell in the middle of them resting as each Daisy placed their inner petal arm around her waist.

It was a long journey that felt would never end and yet to their astonishment they were suddenly looking down on a brightly lit familiar garden, which not only had fairy lights around Fairy Glen but fairy lights around a conservatory, a lily pond, a garden seat, a small bridge, an arch, and a wild flower garden. Two fairy elders flew to greet them and to make sure they could land safely, they knew in advance how weak Snowbell had become and were concerned that the two daisies that had just earned their legs and wings ready to be anointed flower fairies, had kind of been thrown into quite a lot of demanding and definitely frightening things. The elders allowed the two Miss Daisy Weeds to complete this incredible task without help from them. They just beckoned the daisies to follow and land where soft moss had been placed for them. It all went without a hitch and as the three sat upright, Snowbell doing her normal smile, sneeze and yawn, the whole array in the garden cheered and clapped. Fairies stood everywhere in the garden, waiting to greet this miraculous little trio of heroes.Clover cried openly, as the love of his life Miss Daisy Weed returned and wriggled his roots so much with excitement that Horace, who had moved into the garden complete with his arthritic mother, fell off Clovers head. He had climbed up earlier when he heard the news and wanted a good view of them landing. Lily lay back in her pond, spectator to all the excellent flying skills these normally routed Miss Daisy Weeds suddenly could do, their technique was quite breath taking as they looped the loop before their perfect landing. It appeared to all in the garden, even Ivy, that it was difficult to imagine them ever without wings and legs.

Snowbell was carried by the elders on a woven grass seat, which was more like a throne and then she was placed in Fairy Glen to recover fully. Snowbell almost danced with glee when she spotted the pile of juicy berries, elderberries, blackberries and grapes [big juicy black ones]. Snowbell almost forgot her manners as her little hands grabbed the biggest grape between them. Snowbell felt heaven-sent, she would eat and eat until her tummy ached and even then she might eat a little more. The elders looked on and laughed as they saw less and less of Snowbell's face and more and more of red grape juice.

"Will you be ready to talk to us after you finish your meal Snowbell," asked a fairy elder, but as Snowbell tried to reply, her eyes closed and she was unable to do anything but sleep. The elder returned to the garden to see what the two daisies were doing. The two Miss Daisy Weeds were sitting, one at either side of Clover."Even with legs and wings I cannot tell you apart, you are certainly one," said Clover.A giggle followed from Horace. "Yes, Sir Clover, they were cloned."

"That is not very nice Horace, in fact it's quite rude and very hurtful," Clover chastised, and for a second Horace looked ashamed and almost ready to cry, until his giggles got the better of him again.

He crawled at speed away and under a stone, where his mother was waiting for him, she had seen some small flying ants and was drooling with the thoughts of them.

Horace still glancing over at his two daisy friends, set about the task of getting his mother safely inside the garden shed behind his web, which was now their home. He then returned to see how many insects he had caught in his new web which he had placed at the back of the shed up to the garden wall. He caught so much in this clever web that both he and his mother were having to watch that they did not put weight on. They loved their new friends and home, his mother said she was the happiest she had ever been. Time was passing and when Snowbell woke, she flew to be near the two daisies, her fear for them on waking was correct as the two daisies were drying out. Snowbell waved her wand, as only she knew how and the tired Daisy wings dropped to their side and started to change into petals. Their legs disappeared and roots wriggled to find the earth to dig deep into, to drink and survive. They were soon deep rooted, one at either side of Clover, their roots touching him for comfort. Snowbell returned to her upturned mushroom, her favorite bed in Fairy Glen and thought of the return of Miss Daisy Weed to the open countryside, where Daisy the cow desperately wanted her return. Daisy had not wanted to go to the milking shed in case she missed her friend's return, in fact she was one very sad cow, even the farmer who had travelled miles to get a different mix of food could not get a smile out of Daisy. Daisy went down the field after milking and lay where Miss Daisy Weed's siblings grew, they were also sad and Daisy the cow tried hard to keep them positive.

"She will return," she mooed, "now wash those dirty faces, all these children, what have I done to deserve all these daisies." She mooed and shook her bell.Daisy the cow who, in her depressed state, had forgotten how to skip with happiness, sauntered down the field after early morning milking. It was a lovely, bright and fresh morning almost with a hint of autumn in the air, yet poor Daisy hardly noticed as she routinely went about her day hoping somehow, today would be the day that Miss Daisy Weed returned."Flies, those dreaded flies, and so early in the morning," she mooed in annoyance. "Don't flick your tail at me my friend," Miss Daisy Weed said as Snowbell placed her on Daisy the cow's back. Snowbell and Miss Daisy Weed had flown together to the open countryside where she lived with Daisy the cow, enjoying her scenic views of fields, hills and the river that brought her to this paradise.

Miss Daisy Weed still had her wings and her legs when she arrived on Daisy the cow's back so when Daisy's tongue shot out in sheer delight as she tried to lick Miss Daisy Weed on her back, Miss Daisy Weed exclaimed:"Do watch my wings and my legs."

Daisy the cow had never seen a flower fairy in the whole of her milking life and so for a few moments she was stunned and could not get a moo out. Miss Daisy Weed had flown and landed on the bridge of the cow's nose and started to do a little dance, each time she slipped she flew back and began to dance and sing in a kind of fairy gig. Daisy the cow, in sheer happiness, skipped and did a kind of cow gig herself. The two friends were so happy to be united once again, never to part, until the next time. Daisy the cow like Clover the flower, was beginning to realize that to keep her best friend Miss Daisy Weed in the earth could be quite a task.